PLANTS VS. ZOMBIES

Brain Busters

By Emily C. Hughes

HARPER FESTIVAL

An Imprint of HarperCollinsPublishers

HarperFestival is an imprint of HarperCollins Publishers.

Plants vs. Zombies: Brain Busters
Text and illustrations © 2013 by Electronic Arts Inc.
Plants vs. Zombies and PopCap are registered trademarks of Electronic Arts Inc.
All rights reserved. Printed in the United States of America.
No part of this book may be used or reproduced in any manner whatsoever without
written permission except in the case of brief quotations embodied in critical articles
and reviews. For information address HarperCollins Children's Books, a division of
HarperCollins Publishers, 10 East 53rd Street, New York, NY 10022.
www.harpercollinschildrens.com
ISBN 978-0-06-222844-4
Designed by Victor Joseph Ochoa
13 14 15 16 17 LP/RRDH 10 9 8 7 6 5 4 3 2 1
❖
First Edition

Answer key for all activities in this book

can be found on pages 214 to 224.

HEY, NEIGHBOR! My name is Dave, and I'm CRRRRAZY! People call me Crazy Dave. Not sure where they came up with that one.

Hope you're enjoying the neighborhood so far! It's a nice place to live. Just one little pest problem—the zombie infestation is wreaking havoc with property values!

Luckily, you've got one thing on your side:

PLANTS!

Zombie Almanac

Here are a few of the zombies you might have to fend off. Fill in the boxes below with how you think each one became a zombie!

Zombie

Newspaper Zombie

Flag Zombie

Conehead Zombie

Buckethead Zombie

Football Zombie

Screen Door Zombie

Pole Vaulting Zombie

Fun-Dead Maze

Uh-oh. The zombies are standing between you and your seeds. Figure out the best way to get through!

START

FINISH

Know Your Peas

Can you name each of these pea-shooting plants? Write your answer in the spaces below.

Peashooter

Split Pea

repeater

three Pea

Gatling Pea

Not for Zombies

Everyone knows that zombies LOVE brains, but what's less well-known are some of the foods that zombies hate. Draw them in!

Brussels sprouts

grape jelly

pancakes

roast chicken

ice-cream sundaes

Not for Me

List the foods that make YOU run away screaming!

1. Peas
2. chicken
3. rice
4. ~~cake~~ cake
5. cup cakes
6.
7.
8.
9.
10.

Fun-Dead Word Search

Find all 12 zombielicious words!

WALL-NUT
BRAINS
JALAPEÑO
ZOMBIE
PLANTS
BACKYARD
PEASHOOTER
ZOMBOSS
STARFRUIT
SUNFLOWER
SQUASH
ROOF

```
D U B P A S Z C J O T S N Z B
Y V E L W T U I A W R Q J O A
J S W A L L N U T A M U Y P C
S E S N X O J P Q Z A A D N K
T P S T L F Z O M B O S S R Y
A G Q S D W O L L K P H C S A
R H V O X D M U L C P I A U R
F J A K D F B R A I N S A N D
R A L F D S I L V F U M B F V
U L K M F Y E Y Z D A A S L I
I A Q H T I H A X N G N J O K
T P E A S H O O T E R F Q W L
L E S B F Z K M K X O E C E U
R N U E B X R D A J O A P R V
C O Z V T D R E O V F M F T E
```

15

Fun-Dead Dreams

When zombies go to bed, do they count brains?
Draw what you think a zombie dream might look like.

Brain
3

Brain
1

Brain
2

Zombie News

What's that Newspaper Zombie so interested in reading, anyway? Write the hard-hitting exposé you'd want to read if YOU were undead.

NEWS STUFF

Zombie

Draw here

Zombies have Been takeing over the city and evory one has been runing away Becaus zombies are taking over the city. No one nos wher they came from the city has gone crazy for Days Becaves of the worrtbl Zombies pleas help us stop them.

Zombie Notes

Those zombies—they're persistent, but they didn't do too well in school. Can you correct some zombie spelling?

Hello,
   We herd u were having a pool party. We think that iz fun. Well be rite over.

                    Sincerely,
                    the Zombies

Hello,
   This iz your muther. Please come over to myhouse for "Meatloaf" Leave yur front doar open and your lawn ungarded.
                    Sincerely,
                    Mom (not the Zombiez)

Hello,
   We wood like to visit for a midnight znack.
   How does ice cream and brains zound?
                    Sincerely,
                    the Zombees

Write your own note back
to the zombies! For an extra
zombie-rrific signature, try signing
your name with the hand you
don't normally write with!

Hi Zombies
You arnt
Very nice
Why cant yo
Be nice
From Ava
to. Zombies

Connect the Dots

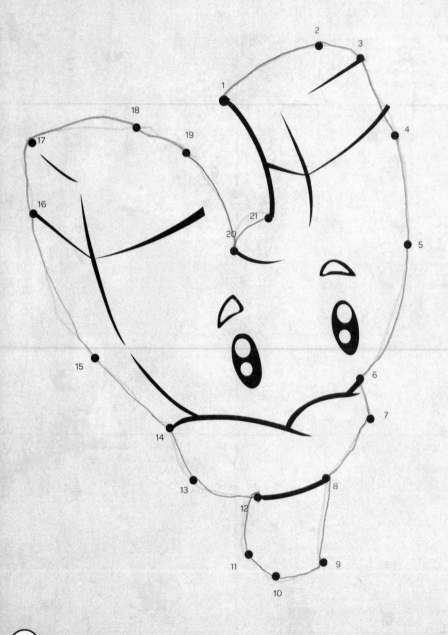

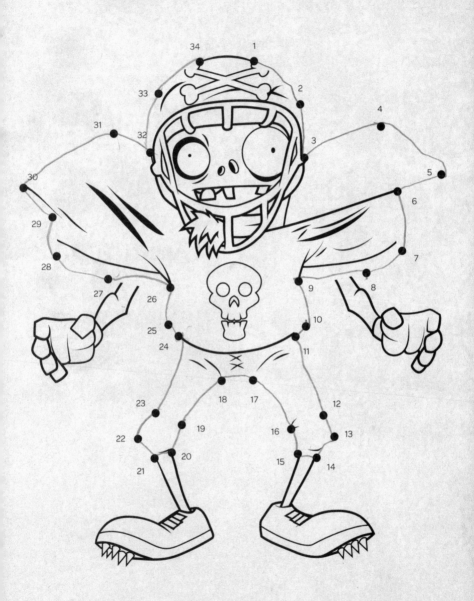

Fun-Dead Word Search

Can you find these types of zombies in the puzzle?

FOOTBALL

POOL

CONEHEAD

NEWSPAPER

FLAG

DANCING

SNORKEL

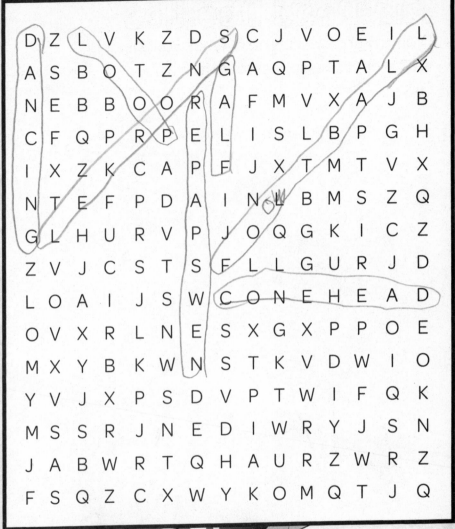

```
D Z L V K Z D S C J V O E I L
A S B O T Z N G A Q P T A L X
N E B B O O R A F M V X A J B
C F Q P R P E L I S L B P G H
I X Z K C A P F J X T M T V X
N T E F P D A I N L B M S Z Q
G L H U R V P J O Q G K I C Z
Z V J C S T S F L L G U R J D
L O A I J S W C O N E H E A D
O V X R L N E S X G X P P O E
M X Y B K W N S T K V D W I O
Y V J X P S D V P T W I F Q K
M S S R J N E D I W R Y J S N
J A B W R T Q H A U R Z W R Z
F S Q Z C X W Y K O M Q T J Q
```

Fun-Dead Doodles

Draw a brand-new zombie. What would it look like? What accessories would it have?

If you were stuck on a zombie-fied desert island, which three plants would you bring with you? Draw 'em in below.

Pea suter

sun Flower

e.N Plant

Sudoku Time!

To play, draw in the boxes below so that every box, every row, and every column has one (and only one!) of each kind of plant.

KEY:

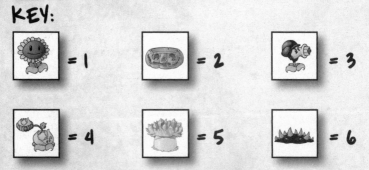

Brain Power

What words can you make using the letters in these words? An example for each is given.

Peashooter

Toes

Torchwood

Door

Grave Buster

Ever

Zombie Almanac

Here are a few more zombies you might have to fend off. Fill in the boxes below with how you think each one became a zombie.

Jack-in-the-Box Zombie

This one ate a Jack in the Box

Dolphin Rider Zombie

This one a a Dolphin

Ducky Tube Zombie

This one ate a Ducky tube

Snorkel Zombie

This one ate a snorkel

Dancing Zombie

This one Plant
Practist
Dance to much

Backup Dancer

Pratist Back
Dancing to
much

Zombie Bobsled Team

Prakest Bobsle
to much

Dr. Zomboss

DiD to much
reeerch on
inventions

Fun-Dead Doodles

The Bloom & Doom Seed Co. is stumped. They need some ideas for new plants—can you help? Draw in your plants and describe what they can do.

Fun-Dead Maze

Crazy Dave has plenty of seeds to sell, but you have to get past the zombies to get to him!

START

FINISH

Can you name the plant upgrades on the packets that Crazy Dave has left?

Cob Connon

winter melon

bandige roll-nont

Gatling Pea

Connect the Dots

37

Zombie Armory

Zombies get pretty creative when it comes to defending themselves from plants. They've got a whole range of armor:

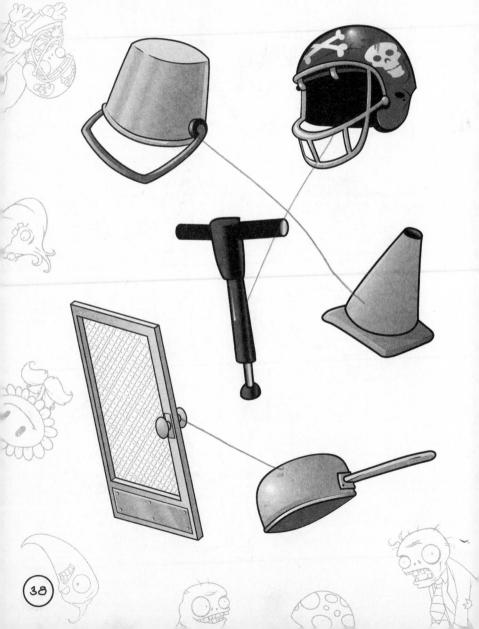

Create the ULTIMATE zombie suit of armor!

Scrambled Brains

Unscramble the words below to find out what plants help fend off the zombie horde.

SNFLUERWO

sunflower

OHMRCBRYEB

_____

RETREEPA

Repeater

HORTOPSAEE

_____

OHLRMSGMOOO

_____

TRFSARTIU

_____

MULPLETNO

_____

TEPARHERETE

Three Peater

ÑOLAPEJA

Jalapeño

SWEEPIDEK

_____

Zombie Almanac

Here are a few more zombies you might have to fend off. Fill in the boxes below with how you think each one became a zombie.

Catapult Zombie

Balloon Zombie

Pogo Zombie

Digger Zombie

Zombie Yeti

Bungee Zombie

Gargantuar

Baseball Zombie

Lawn Mower Maze

Uh-oh. You're out of plants! The lawn mower is your last line of defense—use it to mow down some zombies!

START

44

FINISH

What words can you make using the letters in

LAWN MOWER

Wow

Lawn

Awe

Spot the Differences

Zombie #1 has all its pieces while Zombie #2 is missing five things! Find what's missing and draw it in on Zombie #2.

Zombie #1

Zombie #2

Fun-Dead Friends

Zombies have very distinct personalities, just like your friends. Which of your friends is most like the zombies listed below?

Flag Zombie

Always the first person to try something new!

_____

Newspaper Zombie

This one hates to be interrupted, especially while reading.

_____

Football Zombie
The star athlete!

_____

Balloon Zombie
This one's always got his head
in the sky.

_____

Dr. Zomboss
The brainiac of the group.

_____

Fun-Dead Word Search

Can you find these types of plants in the puzzle?

CHERRY BOMB

POTATO MINE

FUME-SHROOM

CHOMPER

DOOM-SHROOM

TORCHWOOD

SPLIT PEA

CABBAGE-PULT

Z	A	D	C	D	M	C	H	O	M	P	E	R	L	P
T	U	U	R	A	A	O	R	L	I	K	Q	O	O	E
P	D	F	Y	C	B	G	O	R	D	Q	A	T	Y	A
R	G	U	X	H	G	B	O	R	E	G	A	A	E	B
H	D	U	N	E	V	F	A	C	H	T	J	P	E	Q
Q	Q	D	S	R	V	Z	N	G	O	S	T	N	V	B
D	G	U	Q	R	R	Z	R	G	M	E	I	M	K	I	W
O	B	D	D	Y	R	H	I	Q	L	P	E	O	N	H
O	M	O	T	B	L	N	P	P	R	F	U	Y	O	U
W	D	W	I	O	E	T	S	B	X	O	Z	L	X	D
H	C	C	J	M	A	C	K	V	V	J	R	B	T	G
C	D	U	V	B	M	O	O	R	H	S	E	M	U	F
R	B	R	L	F	Y	W	R	M	L	U	P	Q	J	A
O	G	X	G	R	V	X	G	Y	G	I	J	Y	R	W
T	K	T	P	L	Z	N	A	I	C	C	V	C	E	X

Mighty Mushrooms

Plant some mushrooms in your garden and you'll be rid of the zombies in no time! Do you know which mushroom is which? Write in their names next to their pictures.

fume-shroom

magnet-shroom

Ice-shroom

Doom-shroom

scardy-shroom

sun-shroom

_____

53

Crazy Dave's Crazy Maze

Uh-oh. Crazy Dave's lost his keys again. Better help him find them or he'll be sleeping on your couch tonight.

START

FINISH

Why is Crazy Dave sad? He's got no body! Draw in his missing items and make him happy.

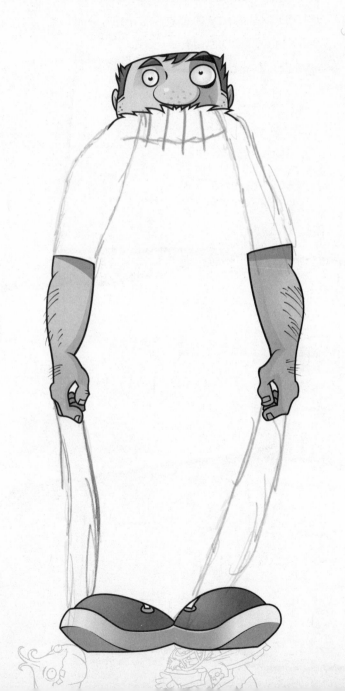

Fun-Dead Notes

Are you right-handed or left-handed? Try writing with
your other hand to copy the zombies' handwriting.
Make sure you spell correctly!

Defense!

It's just you and some very hungry Football Zombies. Better hustle!

START

FINISH

More Sudoku

To play, draw in the boxes below so that every box, every row, and every column has one (and only one!) of each kind of plant.

KEY:

Plant for Your Life!

See how fast you can draw in all the plants you'll need to fend off those zombies—don't take longer than three minutes or your brains'll be in danger!

Zombie Backstory

What were these zombies up to before they decided to launch an all-out assault on your yard? Draw a day in the life of a zombie below.

Title

MORNING

NOON

NIGHT

61

Zombie News

Football Zombie gives 110% whenever he's on the field, even though he doesn't know what a football is. Write a newspaper article about Football Zombie: Did he win the big brain? Did he go home hungry? Get creative!

Title

By

Draw here

Draw here

Draw here

Family Album Time!

Draw the following plants when they were just seedlings. For extra embarrassment, make sure you give them nicknames. (It's okay, you can admit that your mom used to call you Snookums. We won't tell.)

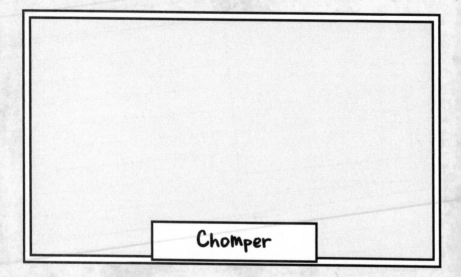

Chomper

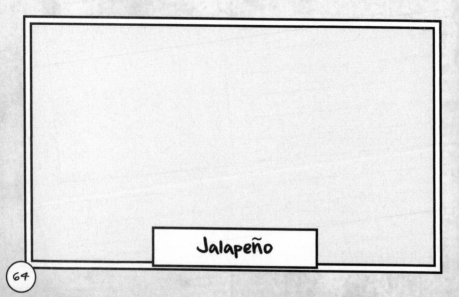

Jalapeño

Melon-pult

Tangle Kelp

Grave Buster

Zombericks!

Can you write zombie limericks? Here's one example:

There once was a zombie from York
Who always ate brains with a fork.
His friends would all laugh
To see such a gaff
And told him he looked like a dork.

In a garden filled with sunflowers

_____

_____

_____

_____

The zombies who never said please

_____

_____

_____

_____

Oh, how I love to eat brains!

_____

_____

_____

_____

When zombies arrive at your door

_____
_____
_____
_____

If ever you find yourself undead

_____
_____
_____
_____

Name That Zombie

What would you name these zombies?

This guy looks like a Melvin.
Yup, definitely a Melvin.

My
Name Was

Hello! My name is
Dancer
zombie

Hello! My name is
ballon
zombie

Hello! My name is
snorkel
zombie

What Are They Thinking?

Plants are known for being pretty private—if they have any opinions, they keep them quiet. Now it's your turn to get inside the mind of some flora. Fill in the thought bubbles for the plants below!

If Zombies Ran the World . . .

It's the zombies' world—we just live in it. When the fun-dead run things, life'll be a little different. What do you think it'll be like to have zombies around in the following roles? Draw these in below.

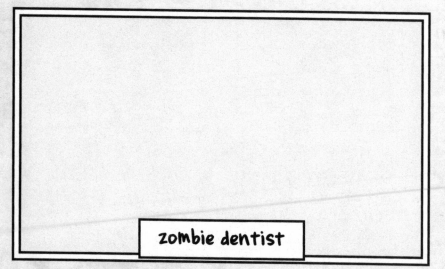

zombie dentist

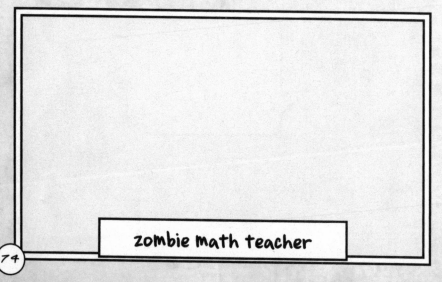

zombie math teacher

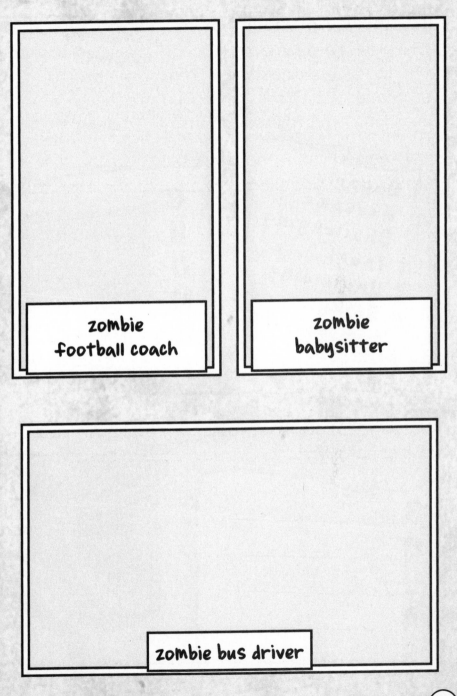

zombie
football coach

zombie
babysitter

zombie bus driver

Power Plants

Your plants have some pretty special characteristics—
why don't you outline some of them below? Next to
each letter of the plant's name, fill in an adjective (a
descriptive word) that starts with that letter—like this!

Capable
Awesome
Challenging
Tough
Unyielding
Spiky

C_____
H_____
O_____
M_____
P_____
E_____
R_____

S__sq_____
Q_____
U_____
A_____
S_____
H_____

W
A
L
L
.
N
U
T
_____

S
T
A
R
F
R
U
I
T
_____

Fun-Dead Doodles

Draw a house that will keep you safe from the zombies.
Where will you place your plants for the best defense
against the horde?

Crossword Time!

ACROSS

2. Collect these to go shopping at Crazy Dave's
3. Don't forget your sunscreen when you plant this
5. A tough one to crack
6. The starting point of any good zombie defense garden
10. Your motorized last line of defense!
11. An icy vehicle for a zombie invasion
12. Home base for your plants

DOWN

1. It's coming for your braaaaains!
2. Neighbor who's off his rocker
4. Spicy and explosive!
7. How'd the zombies get up here, anyway?
8. The zombies are after yours
9. Watery battleground

Crossword answers:

1. (down) zombie
2. (across) coins
3. (across) sunflower
4. (down) jalapeno
5. (across) wallnut
6. (across) fien
7. (down) roof
8. (down) Brains
9. (down) pool
10. (across)
11. (across) bobsled
12. (across) l

Sudoku Time!

To play, draw in the boxes below so that every box, every row, and every column has one (and only one!) of each kind of plant.

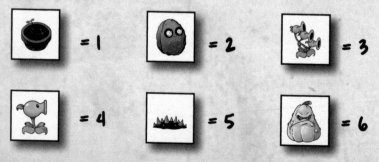

KEY:

= 1   = 2   = 3

= 4   = 5   = 6

Fun-Dead Dreams

When a zombie's coming for you, there's only one thing on its mind—your brains! Draw what your brains look like to a hungry zombie.

Fun-Dead Doodles

How's your drawing hand? Practice your skills
by copying the zombie below!

Scribblemania!

Make a scribble—like this:

Then turn it into something else entirely—like this!

Scribble away! What can you do with this one?
Be sure to tell the world what it is!

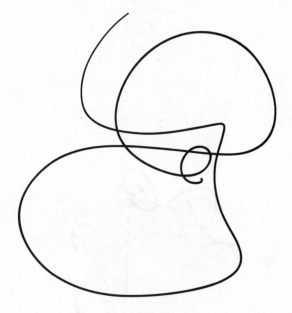

Fun-Dead Doodles

Crazy Dave's got his own unique style—crazy shoes, crazy pot helmet, crazy eyes. It's crazy chic. How would you dress for the zombie apocalypse? Draw a couple outfits below!

Spot the Differences

Zombie #1 has all its pieces while Zombie #2 is missing five things! Find what's missing and draw it in on Zombie #2.

Zombie #1

ZOMBEY

Zombie #2

Fun-Dead Word Search

Find the following words!

GROAN

UNDEAD

ZOMBIE

GNAW

BUNGEE

MOAN

BRAINS

CONEHEAD

POOL

ROTTING

LIMBS

BACKYARD

```
P Y H M W R S L H Q T V N Z R
K F D U G L I F P E D X U Z A
J S W A R L N U T A M U Y O C
S E S C O N E H E A D A D M K
P O O L A Z O M B O L I M B S
G Q S P N G E W N L F S I I X
R H V O X D M G L C P M A E B
F J A B D F B N A I N O A N R
R A L U N D E A D F U A B F A
P H D N F Y E W Z D A N S L I
L A Q G T I H A X N G N J O N
T P E E S H P H T F O V M R S
L E S E F Z K M K X O E C E U
R N U E B X P R O T T I N G V
C O B A C K Y A R D F M F T E
```

Fun-Dead Dreams

A zombie's worst nightmare is a lawn full of plants in between it and your brains. Draw this zombie's bad dream garden below!

Scribblemania!

Enjoy one minute of endless scribbles.

Sudoku Time!

To play, draw in the boxes below so that every box, every row, and every column has one (and only one!) of each kind of zombie.

KEY:

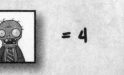 = 1

 = 2

 = 3

= 4

 = 5

 = 6

Junk in the Trunk

Welcome to Crazy Dave's Twiddydinkies! He's got some pretty useful stuff in here—what else would you like to see for sale?

Zombie News

Nobody knows this zombie invasion better than you and Crazy Dave—and it's your civic duty to let the rest of your town know how to protect their brains. Write an article for your town newspaper.

NEWS STUFF

By _____

Draw here

Draw here

Draw here

Connect the Dots

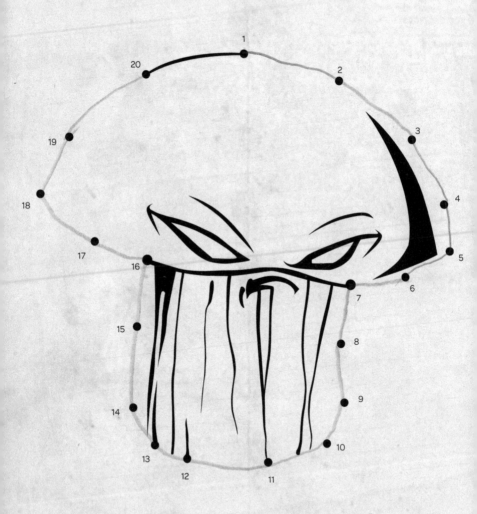

Scrambled Brains

Unscramble the words below. Some are plants and some are zombie names.

APNEKGELTL

_____

TNULALT

_Tall nut_____

TWOODCRHO

_Torchwood_____

ELVULRPOATE

_____

TASHACRN

_____

KRSOELN

_____

AFLG

flag
_____

EDEOCHNA

_____

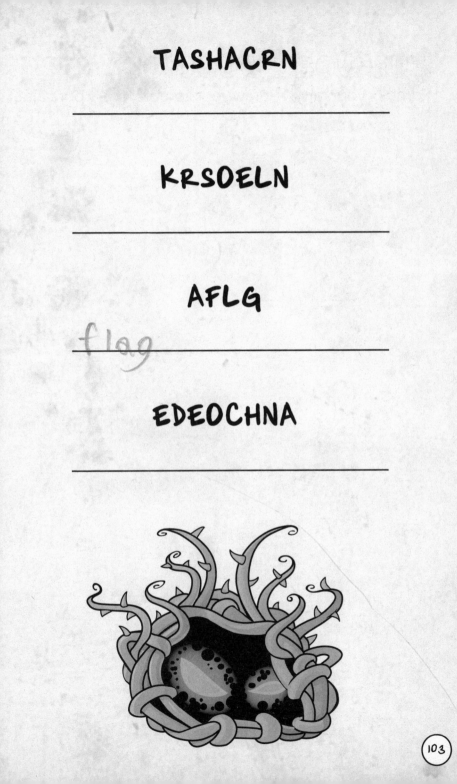

Fun-Dead Doodles

Zombify your family—draw your zombie family portraits!

Brain Power

List some adjectives for the zombies below—can you think of more than five for each zombie?

1. _____
2. _____
3. _____
4. _____
5. _____

1. _____
2. _____
3. _____
4. _____
5. _____

1. _____
2. _____
3. _____
4. _____
5. _____

1. _____
2. _____
3. _____
4. _____
5. _____

1. _____
2. _____
3. _____
4. _____
5. _____

1. _____
2. _____
3. _____
4. _____
5. _____

107

Fun-Dead Doodles

Can you follow the lines? Try copying the plant below!

Fun-Dead Doodles

Uh-oh. A huge wave of zombies is approaching—better put together your defense! Sketch in which plants you'd use to defend the house!

Fun-Dead Doodles

Draw the plant that best defeats each zombie.

Fun-Dead Word Search

Find the words below in the puzzle.

CRAZY DAVE

TWIDDYDINKIES

BLOOM

DOOM   SNOW PEA

SEED PACKET   CONEHEAD

ZOMBIE   GARDEN

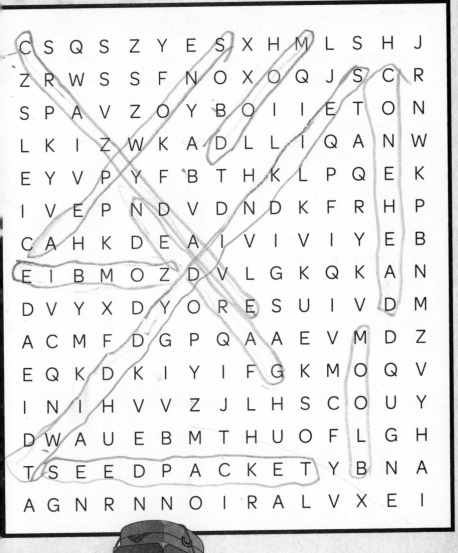

```
C S Q S Z Y E S X H M L S H J
Z R W S S F N O X O Q J S C R
S P A V Z O Y B O I I E T O N
L K I Z W K A D L L I Q A N W
E Y V P Y F B T H K L P Q E K
I V E P N D V D N D K F R H P
C A H K D E A I V I V I Y E B
E I B M O Z D V L G K Q K A N
D V Y X D Y O R E S U I V D M
A C M F D G P Q A A E V M D Z
E Q K D K I Y I F G K M O Q V
I N I H V V Z J L H S C O U Y
D W A U E B M T H U O F L G H
T S E E D P A C K E T Y B N A
A G N R N N O I R A L V X E I
```

TU POD

Fun-Dead Doodles

Crazy Dave uses that pot as a helmet, and so far it seems to be keeping him pretty safe. What other household items could you use for zombie defense? Draw them in.

Zombie Trivia

Zombie facts—write in some little-known zombie trivia below.

1. _____

2. _____

3. _____

4. Dancing Zombies hate disco— they much prefer polka!

5. _____

6. _____

7. Contrary to popular belief, Conehead Zombie isn't a stickler for traffic safety—he just really loves to party.

8. _____

9. _____

10. _____

11._____

12. Digger Zombie spends three days a week getting his excavation permits in order.

13._____

14._____

15._____

Spot the Differences

Zombie #1 has all its pieces while Zombie #2 is missing five things! Find what's missing and draw it in on Zombie #2.

Zombie #1

Zombie #2

Scribblemania!

Turn these scribbles into masterpieces!

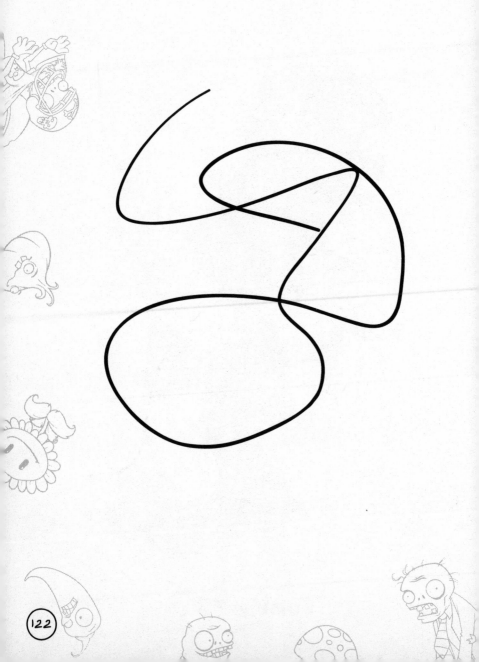

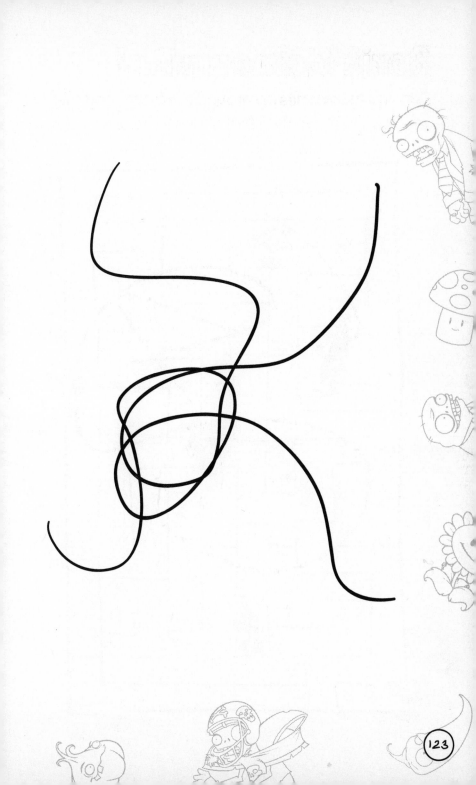

Zombie Snowmen!

Can you make your way around the frozen zombies on your lawn? Use the chilly plants to help!

START

FINISH

Brain Power

What words can you make out of . . .

WINTER MELON

Lion

ICE-SHROOM

Rice

Fun-Dead Friends

Match your friends to their plant counterparts!

Peashooter: Old reliable— you can always count on him to come through in a pinch.

_____

Jalapeño: This one's got a temper, and when it blows, he takes care of all problems at once.

_____

Tall-nut: His height makes him star of the basketball team.

_____

Split Peas: These two best friends always have each other's backs. _____
and _____

Sudoku Time!

To play, draw in the boxes below so that every box, every row, and every column has one (and only one!) of each kind of plant.

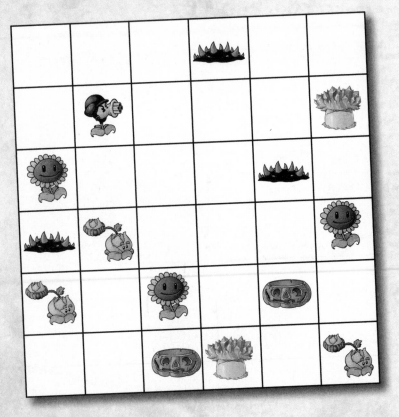

KEY:

128

Scribblemania!

Create another masterpiece using your brainz.

Fun-Dead Doodles

The Dancing Zombie and his Backup Dancers need some new dancers. Draw in some more Dancing Zombies to make the group bigger.

Fun-Dead Doodles

Draw your favorite zombie from memory. No peeking!

FarT HCD)

Brain Power

What words can you make from the letters in

PLANTS VS. ZOMBIES

_____ Pies _____   _____

_____   _____

_____   _____

_____   _____

_____   _____

_____   _____

_____   _____

_____   _____

_____   _____

_____   _____

_____   _____

_____   _____

_____   _____

_____   _____

_____   _____

Crossword Time!

How well do you know your zombie types?

ACROSS

2. Batter's up!
4. Swimming sensation with an aquatic acquaintance
5. Traffic director
8. He's got the moves
9. Leader of the pack—the _____-bearer!
12. This one's a breeze
13. BOOOOIIIIIING!
14. The big boss and brains of the operation
15. He doesn't need it to breathe—it's just an accessory
16. Social climber

DOWN

1. This one's light-headed
3. Up, down, up, down, up, down
6. Reading fiend—or maybe he's doing the crossword?
7. This guy likes to jump
10. If you can't go through, go under
11. Hut! Hut! Hike!

2. baseball

4. snorkel

5.

8. Dancer

12.

14. zomboss

15.

16.

9.

13.

Fun-Dead Maze

You're in the pool, when suddenly—zombies! Dodge them on your way back to the house.

START

FINISH

Fun-Dead Doodles

Your brain is your most prized body part—
draw a loving portrait of it below!

Fun-Dead Doodles

How many different types of plants can you draw from memory? Try for more than fifteen!

Brain Scramble

Unscramble the words below. There are plants, zombies, and more!

DEGNAR

Danger

WSRO

Rows

WALN

Lawn

AUKCDHBEET BIMEZO

Bucket head zombie

GOOP IZEBOM

Pogo Zombie

RD. ZSOBOMS

Dr. Zomboss

ATARGGANUR

Gangan†

Fun-Dead Doodles

What if all zombies were teeny-tiny? Draw tiny versions of the zombies below and find out.

Fun-Dead Poems

A haiku is a three-line poem with five syllables in the first line, seven in the second line, and five in the third line. Here's an example:

> Zombies just love brains.
> Problem is, they love yours too.
> Put your helmet on.

Try writing a couple of your own!

Zombie Jokes

They're drop-dead hilarious!

Q. Who did the zombie take out for dinner?

A. His GHOULfriend!

Q. Where do most zombies live?

A. On dead-end streets.

Q. Where is the safest place in your house to hide from a zombie?

A. The living room.

Q. What do zombies wear to keep dry?

A. BRAINcoats!

Q. What is black, white, and dead all over?

A. A zombie in a tuxedo.

Name That Zombie

Time to name some more zombies. This Dancing Zombie over here? We think his name's Chaz.

What Are They Thinking?

What are these zombies thinking? Fill in the thought bubbles below.

Twiddydinky Doodles

Crazy Dave sells useful stuff out of his car. If you were Dave, what would you sell and how much would you charge for it?

bloom

153

Fun-Dead Zombies

Zombies have a pretty wide range of jobs—miner, snorkeler, pogo-er. What other jobs can you imagine zombies having? Dress these zombies up for their new gigs.

Plant Pet Names

Some people name their pets, but you? You name your plants. Give these little guys some names, like Pete the Peashooter and Wally Wall-nut.

Hello! My name is _____

Hello! My name is _____

Hello! My name is _____

Plant Doodles

Get ready to doodle your plants! Draw new plant ideas here.

Seeder

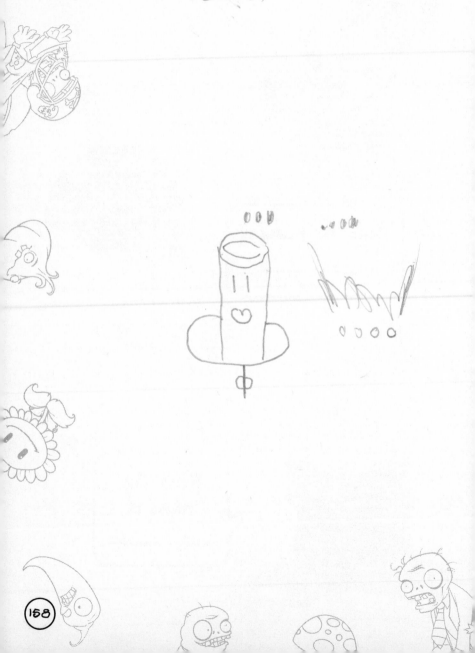

Fun-Dead Doodles

The zombies have many tools to help them get to you—
pogo sticks, dolphins—you name it! What other modes
of transportation could the zombies use? Draw them in
here.

All About You

You know plenty about the plants and zombies. Now tell us a little about yourself!

NICKNAME:

Greg

BIRTHDAY:

4/18/2005

FAVORITE FOOD:

Pizza

FAVORITE BAND:

FAVORITE BOOK EVER:

Super Buddies

PLACE YOU'D MOST LIKE TO TRAVEL:

O's game

MOST EMBARRASSING MOMENT:

FAVORITE ACTOR:

FAVORITE ACTRESS:

_____

PETS:

_____

BEST FRIEND:

_____

BIGGEST FEAR:

_____

YOUR SECRET TALENT:

_____

FAVORITE MONTH:

April
_____

Scribblemania!

Even more scribblemania! Yes way!

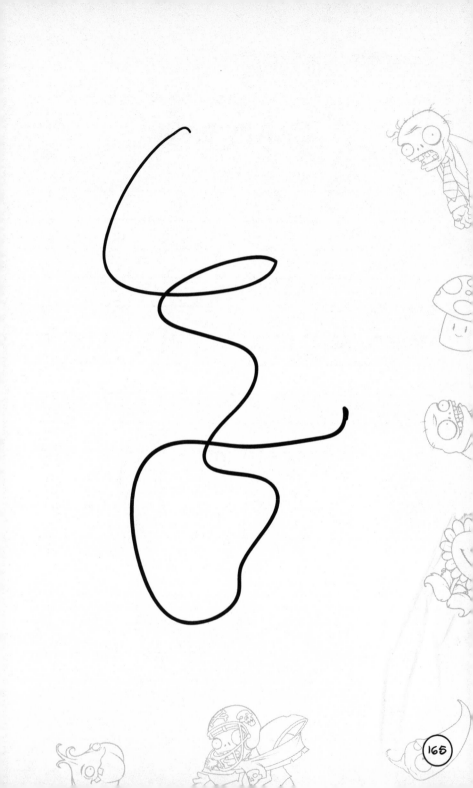

Brain Power

What words can you make from the letters in

CRAZY DAVE

_____ Day _____   _____

_____   _____

_____   _____

_____   _____

_____   _____

_____   _____

_____   _____

_____   _____

_____   _____

_____   _____

_____   _____

_____   _____

_____   _____

_____   _____

_____   _____

_____   _____

How about the letters in Crazy Dave's

TWIDDYDINKIES

_____Dine_____   _____

_____   _____

_____   _____

_____   _____

_____   _____

_____   _____

_____   _____

_____   _____

_____   _____

_____   _____

_____   _____

_____   _____

_____

_____

_____

_____

Fun-Dead Doodles

The zombies all have jobs—but what about you? What do you want to be when you grow up? Draw it below.

Zombies at Work

List ten dream jobs for the zombies:

1. _____

2. _____

3. _____

4. _____

5. _____

6. _____

7. _____

8. _____

9. _____

10. _____

Plant Sudoku

To play, draw in the boxes below so that every box, every row, and every column has one (and only one!) of each kind of plant.

KEY:

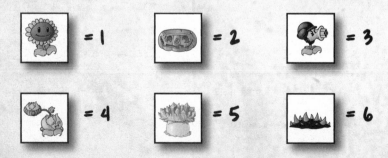

Fun-Dead Scribbles

Create another masterpiece out of this scribble.

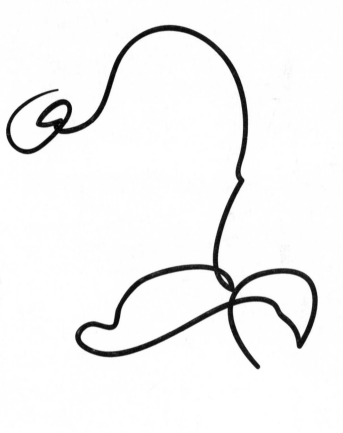

Connect the Dots

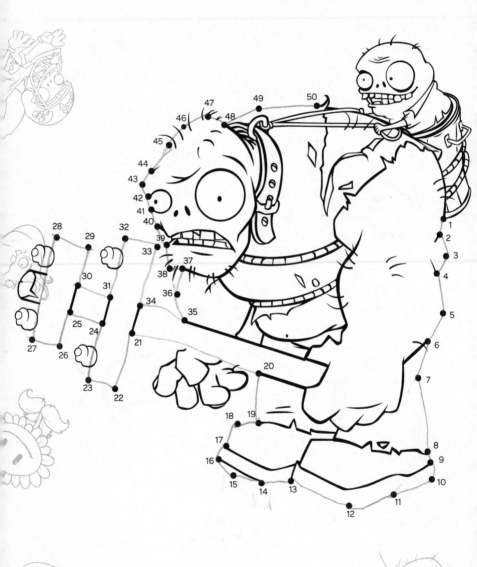

NEWS-STUFF
ZOMBIES!

Monsterful Movies

Draw movie posters using Football Zombie and Flag Zombie. What would these movies be called?

Roof Maze

You're caught on the roof! What were you doing up there, anyway? Make it back to your chimney while dodging those pesky zombies!

START

FINISH

Fun-Dead Dreams

If zombies could grow brains in a garden, what would that garden look like? Draw it here.

Defensive Doodles

The zombies are coming—sketch in which plants you'd use to defend the house!

Sleepytime Doodles

Draw yourself as a sleeping plant.

Sleepy Head

Draw yourself as a sleeping zombie.

One Nut Is Not Like the Other

Wall-nuts and Tall-nuts—so similar, and yet so different. Apart from their heights, they could be one and the same, but they hate being mistaken for each other. List the characteristics that set these two apart!

Tall-nut

_____

_____

_____

Writes poetry in his spare time

_____

Wall-nut

Hates chocolate pudding

Pea Pairing Doodles

Split Peas are stuck together 24/7—that has to be tiring! Imagine if you and your best friend were stuck back to back. Draw it below!

Scribblemania!

What will you think of next?

Connect the Dots

189

Fun-Dead Doodles

How to draw a zombie: step by step!

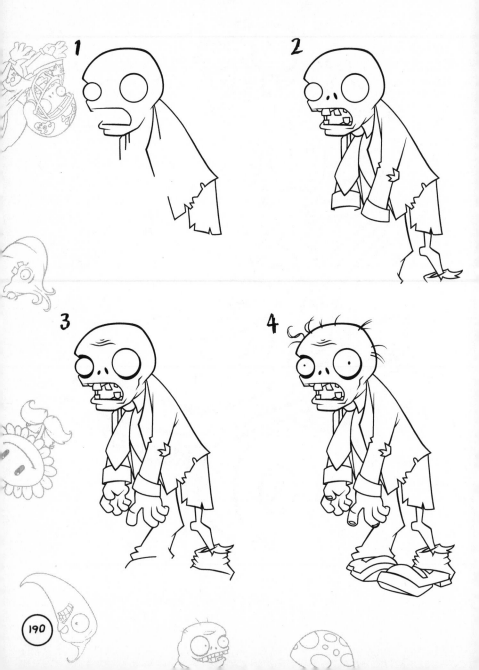

Fun-Dead Doodles

Magnet-shroom can attract anything metal—buckets, helmets, etc. What would you do if you were magnetic? Draw your adventures!

Spot the Differences

Chomper #1 has all its pieces while Chomper #2 is missing five things! Find what's missing and draw it in on Chomper #2.

Chomper #1

Chomper #2

Fun-Dead Doodles

Draw the perfect garden to defend against any zombie—and look nice!

Zombie Maze

Darn—it's foggy again. Luckily you've got a Plantern with you—use it to find your way home!

START

FINISH

Fun-Dead Grooves

Dancing Zombie and its Backup Dancers have some cool moves. Can you think of five fun-dead names for their dancing?

1. _____
2. _____
3. _____
4. _____
5. _____

Scribblemania!

More masterpieces to create!

Crossword Time!

ACROSS

2. Prickly yet lovable!
6. What happens when you put your veggies in the freezer
8. Get rid of those pesky headstones
9. Make sure to eat your peas!
12. Anyone feel a breeze?
13. The taller brother
14. Meeee-ow!

DOWN

1. He's got a sunny disposition
3. Twins with an explosive temper
4. He attacks from below
5. His name is what he does
7. Add a little fire to your power
10. Five points, more protection!
11. You've got some watermelon on your face

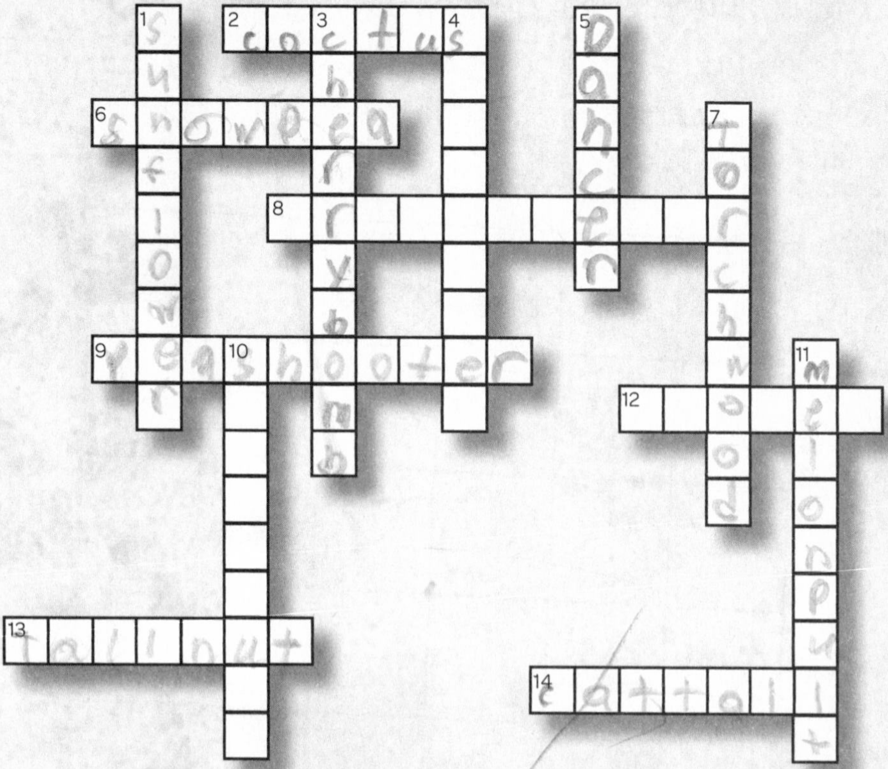

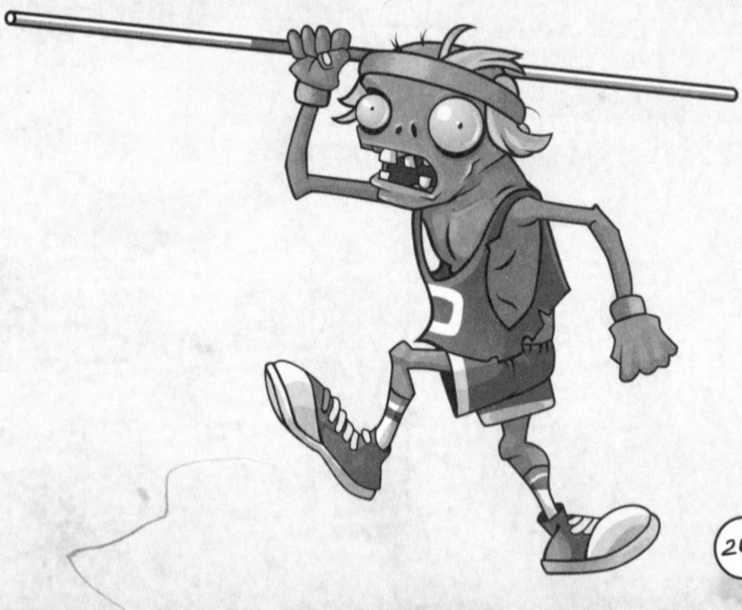

Plant Sudoku

To play, draw in the boxes below so that every box, every row, and every column has one (and only one!) of each kind of plant.

KEY:

Crazy Dave's Confused Maze

Uh-oh. Crazy Dave's lost again. Better go get him.

START

FINISH

Brain Power

What words can you make from the letters in

Zombie Almanac

Maze

Conehead

Need

Gargantuar

Aunt

Screen Door

Reed

Scribblemania!

One last time! What can you create?

Fun-Dead Doodles

Having fun Yeti? Try copying this zombie:

Crazy Dave here! You made it! That's CRRRRAZY! The zombies are defeated. Draw yourself a trophy for making it through and saving your brainz!

Answer Key

Page 10:
Fun-Dead Maze

Page 11:
Know Your Peas

 Peashooter

 Repeater

 Gatling Pea

 Split Pea

 Threepeater

Pages 14-15:
Fun-Dead Word Search

```
D U B P A S Z C J O T S N Z B
Y V E L W T U I A W R Q J O A
J S W A L L N U T A M U Y P C
S E S N X O J P Q Z A A D N K
T P S T L F Z O M B O S S R Y
A G Q S D W O L L K P H C S A
R H V O X D M U L C P I A U R
F J A K D F B R A I N S A N D
R A L F D S I L V F U M B F V
U L K M F Y E Y Z D A A S L I
I A Q H T I H A X N G N J O K
T P E A S H O O T E R F Q W L
L E S B F Z K M K X O E C E U
R N U E B X R D A J O A P R V
C O Z V T D R E O V F M F T E
```

Page 20:
Connect the Dots

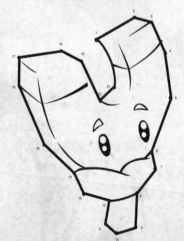

214

Page 21:
Connect the Dots

Pages 22–23:
Word Search Time

```
D Z L V K Z D S C J V O E I L
A S B O T Z N G A Q P T A L X
N E B B O O R A F M V X A J B
C F Q P R P E L I S L B P G H
I X Z K C A P F J X T M T V X
N T E F P D A I N L B M S Z Q
G L H U R V P J O Q G K I C Z
Z V J C S T S F L L G U R J D
L O A I J S W C O N E H E A D
O V X R L N E S X G X P P O E
M X Y B K W N S T K V D W I O
Y V J X P S D V P T W I F Q K
M S S R J N E D I W R Y J S N
J A B W R T Q H A U R Z W R Z
F S Q Z C X W Y K O M Q T J Q
```

Page 26:
Sudoku Time!

Page 34:
Fun-Dead Maze

Page 35:

Melon-pult

Gatling Pea

Cob Cannon

Wall-nut First Aid

Page 36:
Connect the Dots

Page 37:
Connect the Dots

Pages 40-41:
Scrambled Brains

Sunflower
Cherry Bomb
Repeater
Peashooter
Gloom-shroom
Starfruit
Melon-pult
Threepeater
Jalapeño
Spikeweed

Page 44:
Lawn Mower Maze

Pages 46–47:
Spot the Differences

Pages 50–51:
Fun-Dead Word Search

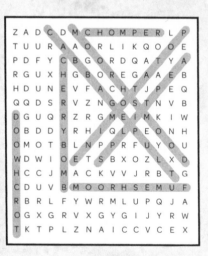

Pages 52–53:
Mighty Mushrooms

 Fume-shroom   Hypno-shroom

 Magnet-shroom   Sun-shroom

 Ice-shroom

 Sea-shroom

 Doom-shroom

 Scaredy-shroom

Page 54:
Crazy Dave's Crazy Maze

Page 57:
Defense!

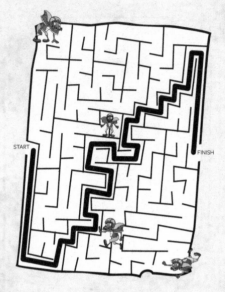

Page 58:
More Sudoku

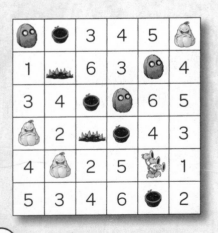

Pages 80-81:
Crossword Time!

ACROSS:
2. Coins
3. Sunflower
5. Wall-nut
6. Seed
10. Lawn Mower
11. Bobsled
12. Flower Pot

DOWN:
1. Zombie
2. Crazy Dave
4. Jalapeño
7. Roof
8. Brains
9. Pool

Page 82:
Sudoku Time!

Pages 90-91:
Spot the Differences

Pages 92-93:
Fun-Dead Word Search

Page 96:
Sudoku Time!

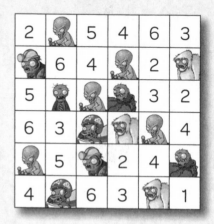

Pages 100-101:
Connect the Dots

Pages 102-103:
Scrambled Brains

Tangle Kelp   Torchwood   Trash Can   Flag

Tall-nut   Pole Vaulter   Snorkel   Conehead

Pages 114-115:
Fun-Dead Word Search

Pages 120-121:
Spot the Differences

Page 124:
Zombie Snowmen!

START

FINISH

Page 128:
Sudoku Time!

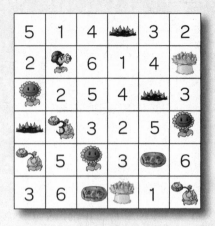

5	1	4	🌱	3	2
2	🧟	6	1	4	🌸
🌻	2	5	4	🌱	3
🌱	🧟	3	2	5	🌻
🌻	5	🌻	3	🎃	6
3	6	🎃	🌸	1	🎃

Pages 134-135:
Crossword Time!

ACROSS:

2. Baseball

4. Dolphin

4. Conehead

8. Dancer

9. Flag

12. Screen Door

13. Bungee

14. Zomboss

15. Snorkel

16. Ladder

DOWN:

1. Balloon

3. Pogo

6. Newspaper

7. Pole Vaulter

10. Digger

11. Football

Page 136:
Fun-Dead Maze

START

FINISH

Pages 140–141: Brain Scramble

Garden
Rows
Lawn
Buckethead Zombie
Pogo Zombie
Dr. Zomboss
Gargantuar

Page 170: Plant Sudoku

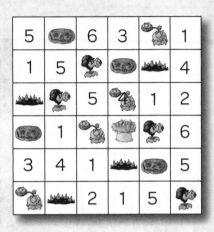

Pages 172–173: Connect the Dots

Page 176:
Roof Maze

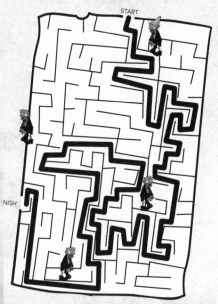

START

NISH

Page 188:
Connect the Dots

Page 189:
Connect the Dots

Pages 194-195:
Spot the Differences

Page 198: Zombie Maze

START

FINISH

Pages 202–203: Crossword Time!

ACROSS:

2. Cactus
6. Snow Pea
8. Grave Buster
9. Peashooter
12. Blover
13. Tall-nut
14. Cattail

DOWN:

1. Sunflower
3. Cherry Bomb
4. Spikeweed
5. Squash
7. Torchwood
10. Starfruit
11. Melon-pult

Page 204: Plant Sudoku

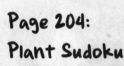

Page 205: Crazy Dave's Confused Maze

START

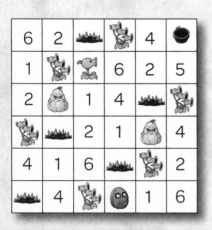

FINISH